This Walker book belongs to:

_____

_____

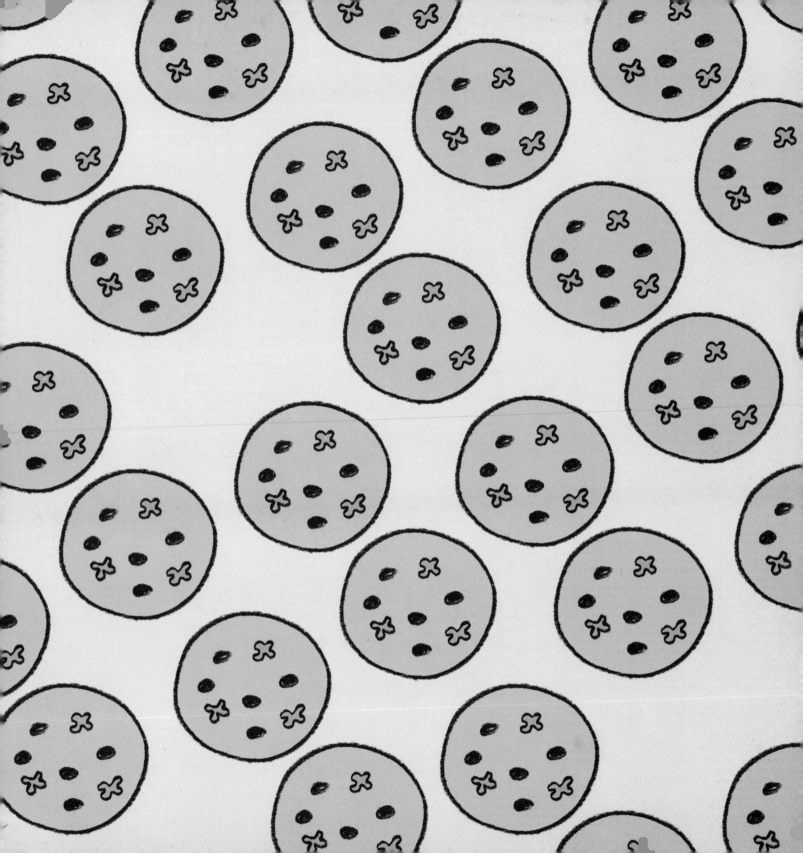

to Cher,
one sweet cookie

I do not like
the look of
that title.

First published in Great Britain 2012 by Walker Books Ltd
87 Vauxhall Walk, London SE11 5HJ

2 4 6 8 10 9 7 5 3 1

Copyright © 2012 Mo Willems

First published in the United States 2012 by Hyperion Books for Children,
an imprint of Disney Book Group. British publication rights arranged with
Wernick & Pratt Agency, LLC.

The right of Mo Willems to be identified as author/illustrator
of this work has been asserted by him in accordance with the
Copyright, Designs and Patents Act 1988.

This book has been handlettered by Mo Willems

Printed in China

British Library Cataloguing in Publication Data:
a catalogue record for this book is available from the British Library.

ISBN 978-1-4063-4009-9

www.walker.co.uk

The Duckling Gets a Cookie!?

words and pictures by mo willems

WALKER BOOKS
AND SUBSIDIARIES
LONDON • BOSTON • SYDNEY • AUCKLAND

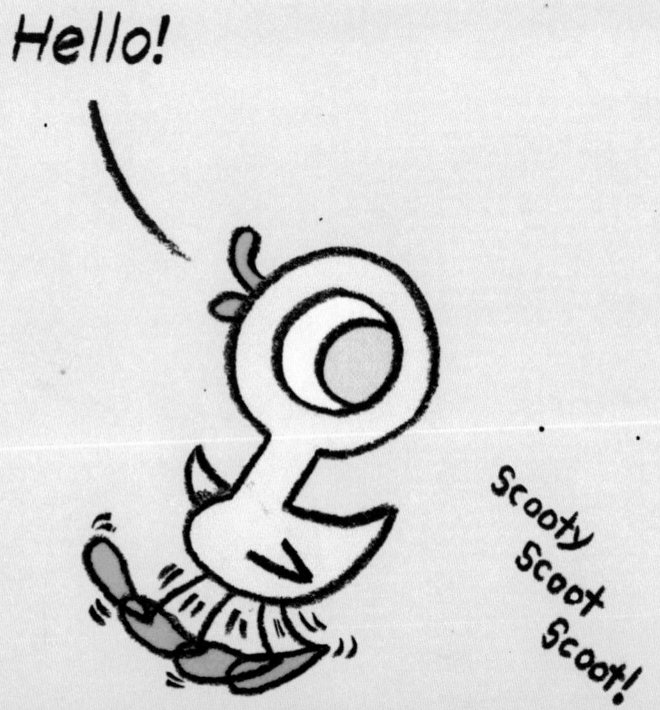
Hello!
Scooty Scoot Scoot!

Oh!

That was very nice
of you!

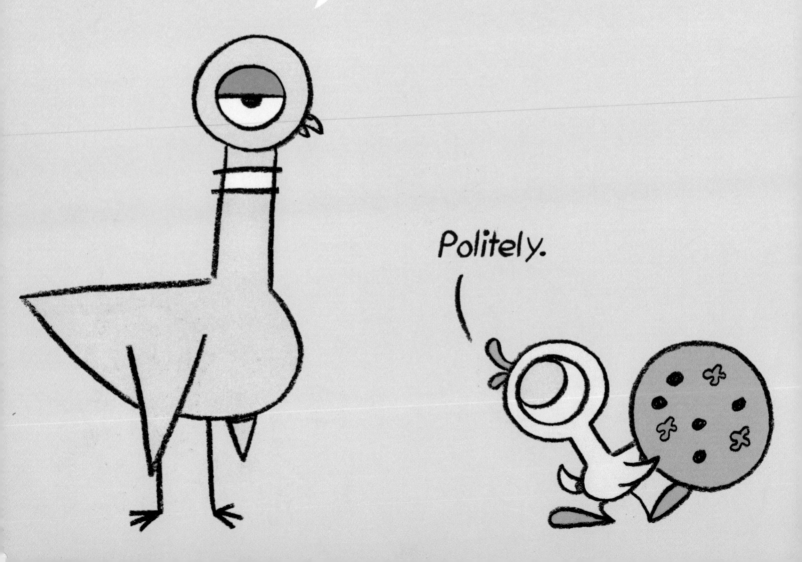

I'll ask for a "Yummy Chip Robot" every now and then.

I've asked for a walrus!

Right now, I'm asking, "Why?"

Why? WHY? WHY?

Pigeons like cookies, too!

(Especially with nuts.)

WHY DID **YOU** GET THAT COOKIE!?!

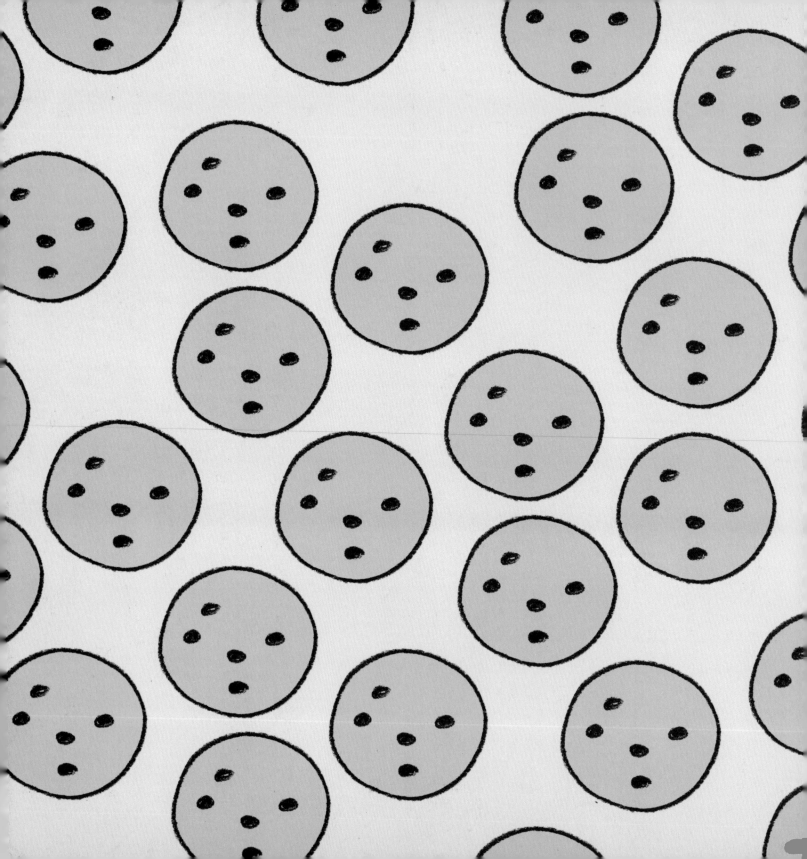

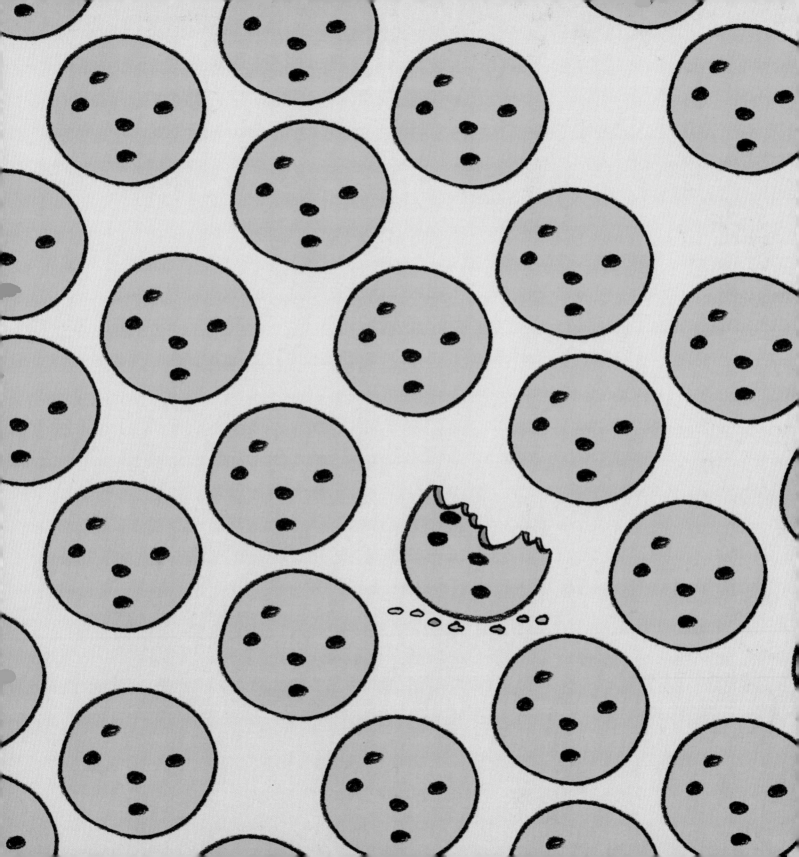

Other books by MO WILLEMS

ISBN: 978-1-84428-545-7

ISBN: 978-1-4063-0812-9

ISBN: 978-1-84428-513-6

ISBN: 978-1-4063-1550-9

ISBN: 978-1-84428-059-9

ISBN: 978-1-4063-1382-6

ISBN: 978-1-4063-3649-8

ISBN: 978-1-4063-1229-4

ISBN: 978-1-4063-1215-7

ISBN: 978-1-4063-0158-8

Available from all good booksellers
www.walker.co.uk